With love for E is for Ellie
and appreciation to the girls, boys, and teachers
at All Children Great and Small

—A.W.P.

Especially for Augie!

—D.W.

Farrar Straus Giroux Books for Young Readers
An imprint of Macmillan Publishing Group, LLC
175 Fifth Avenue, New York, NY 10010

Text copyright © 2019 by Ann Whitford Paul
Pictures copyright © 2019 by David Walker
Color separations by Bright Arts (H.K.) Ltd.
Printed in China by Toppan Leefung Printing Ltd., Dongguan City, Guangdong Province
Designed by Aram Kim
First edition, 2019
1 3 5 7 9 10 8 6 4 2

mackids.com

Library of Congress Cataloging-in-Publication Data

Names: Paul, Ann Whitford, author. | Walker, David, 1965- illustrator.
Title: If animals went to school / Ann Whitford Paul ; pictures by David
  Walker.
Description: First edition. | New York : Farrar Straus Giroux, 2019. |
  Summary: Illustrations and simple, rhyming text follow different members
  of the animal kingdom as they experience a day at school.
Identifiers: LCCN 2018004949 | ISBN 9780374309022 (hardcover)
Subjects: | CYAC: Stories in rhyme. | Schools—Fiction. | Animals—Habits and
  behavior—Fiction.
Classification: LCC PZ8.3.P273645 Ifw 2019 | DDC [E]—dc23
LC record available at https://lccn.loc.gov/2018004949

Our books may be purchased in bulk for promotional, educational, or business use.
Please contact your local bookseller or the Macmillan Corporate and Premium Sales Department
at (800) 221-7945 ext. 5442 or by email at MacmillanSpecialMarkets@macmillan.com.

If Animals Went to School

Ann Whitford Paul

Pictures by David Walker

Farrar Straus Giroux
New York

If animals went to school,
Beaver's papa would tug him.
"You're moving too slow."

But he'd shuf-shuffle-shuffle.
"I don't want to go."

Kangaroo would **jumpity-jump-jump** past
and be first to the room.

Welcome

Beaver?
The last.

Teacher Ms. Cheetah
would stand by the door *purr-purring*,
"Welcome. Let's sit on the floor."

They'd start with a song. She'd **toot-toot** on her flute.

Dingo would **ho-owl** and

Owl **hooty-hoot-hoot**.

Then they'd write their letters,

Panda a **P**,

Cobra a **C**,

Tortoise a **T**.

If animals went to school,

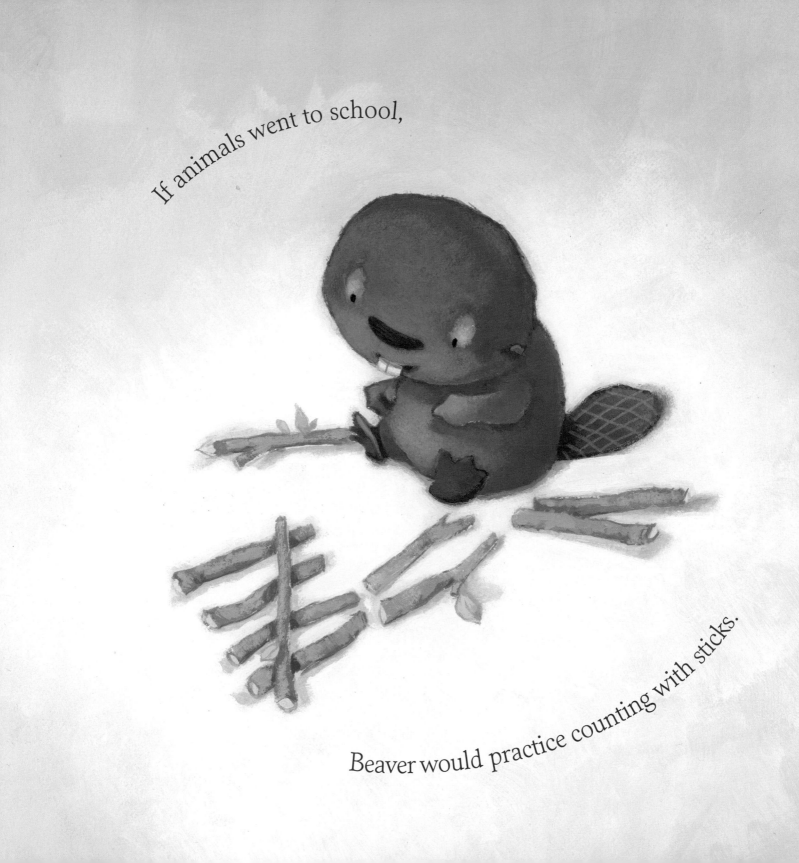

Beaver would practice counting with sticks.

Elephant would add up the cardboard bricks he'd stacked in a tower.

Gator's tail would **thrash-thrash**.

Smack, SMACK

rum-tumble

uh-oh!

CRASH!

Mouse would play with shapes—
a circle, a square.

Who'd hog the triangles?
Grrrrrrrrr, growling Bear!

Fox would rush to the story nook,
and **bark-bark**, "Goat! Stop eating that book."

Teacher Ms. Cheetah would purr, "Time for lunch."

Beaver would **chomp**,

Donkey **munch-munch**.

If animals went to school,
outside Beaver and Skunk would dig
one hole together, humongously big.

Lemur would climb up the tree jungle gym,

and **leap, leap, leap** from limb to limb.

Flamingo would flap
her wings and flounce.
Panda would bounce the ball,

bounce-bounce.

Lemming would **bump!**
on Camel's hump ride.
Goose would glide **wheeeeee!**
down Giraffe's neck slide.

If animals went to school,
Teacher Ms. Cheetah would finally purr,
"That's all for today."

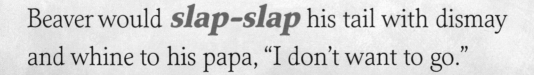

Beaver would **slap-slap** his tail with dismay
and whine to his papa, "I don't want to go."

And he'd shuf-shuffle, shuffle, shuf-shuffle home slooooo-ooooow.